Julius

**The
Perfectly
Pesky
Pet
Parrot**

D0896391

VeraLee Wiggins

Pacific Press Publishing Association
Boise, Idaho
Oshawa, Ontario, Canada

Edited by Aileen Andres Sox
Designed by Dennis Ferree
Cover and inside art by Mary Rumford
Typeset in 14/17 New Century Schoolbook

Library of Congress Cataloging-in-Publication Data:

Wiggins, VeraLee, 1928-
    Julius, the perfectly pesky pet parrot / VeraLee
Wiggins.
        p.   cm.
    Summary: With the help of his pet parrot, Mitch
makes some important discoveries about friendship,
responsibility, and love.
    ISBN 0-8163-1173-0
    [1. Parrots. 2. Pets. 3. Christian life.] I. Title.
PZ7.W6386Ju   1994
[E]—dc20   93-14254
                                                CIP
                                                 AC

94 95 96 97 98 ● 5 4 3 2 1

Dedication

This one's for you, Lisa,

my very own precious bookworm.

I love you forever—

and more each day.

Contents

"Ouch!

Oh—help, Mom, quick!

Julius is biting me."

CHAPTER

1

Mitch Gets a Pet

"Mom!" Mitch Sinclair called, slamming the front door. "Uncle Daryl just dropped me off. Come see what he gave me."

Hearing Mitch's excited call, Mom ran in from the kitchen. She wiped her hands on a small towel folded over her shoulder. When she saw the large green bird and monstrous (really big) cage, her mouth opened into a perfect circle. She was so surprised, she couldn't talk. Wordlessly, she stabbed a finger in the direction of the cage.

"It's Julius, Mom," Mitch said. His voice sounded extra happy. "Remember? Uncle Daryl's parrot. Since he is moving to Maryland, he said I can have Julius. Isn't that neat?"

Mom stood still, hands on hips, feet apart. She didn't say a word.

"Isn't it, Mom? He won't be a lot of work like a cat or dog." Mitch grinned. His eyes danced.

Mom shook her dark head. "I don't know, Mitch."

"I'll do all the work, Mom, and he can live in my room."

"Do you know what parrots eat?" Mom asked.

"Sure, Uncle Daryl told me. And he gave me a big bag of food. It's a mixture of raw peanuts, sunflower seeds, corn, and other grains. Oh, yes, it has chili peppers in it too."

Mom didn't look very convinced. "All right," she said, "take him to your room. But a pet is a big responsibility, Mitch. It's not like a toy that you can put into a drawer until you want to play with it again. God wants us to take good care of any animals we have. You'll have to get up earlier in the mornings to care for him before you go to school."

"I will, Mom. I'll take the very best care of him. And don't worry, you won't even know he's here."

Mitch put the four-foot-tall cage on the floor in the corner of the room. That huge cage sure made the room look smaller.

"Hello-hello-hello," a scratchy voice squawked from the cage.

Mitch grinned all over his face and squatted beside the cage. "Hello, Julius."

"Hello, hello, hello."

"What else do you say, Julius?"

"Hello, hello, hello."

Mitch ran after Mom. "Come hear Julius talk," he insisted.

"Awk! Awk! Awk!" Julius screamed at ear-splitting volume.

Mom put her hands over her ears. Julius screamed again. "That's enough, Mitch," Mom said, shouting to make herself heard. "I don't want to hear anymore."

"OK, Julius, that's enough," Mitch repeated. "Julius! Stop."

"Awk! Awk! Awk!" Julius screamed on and on and on.

"Let's get out of here," Mitch said. "Maybe he'll shut up if we go. Maybe he doesn't like you. He talked before you came in."

"Maybe I don't like him, either," Mom said, hurrying out of the room.

Mitch followed her out and closed the door behind them. The racket followed them all through the house and into the kitchen.

"I know," Mitch said, after Julius screeched for five more minutes, "he's probably thirsty. I'll take him a fresh drink of water."

A few minutes later he opened the cage door and reached in to attach the water dish to the side of the cage.

Before Mitch had the dish in place, Julius hooked onto his arm just below the elbow, causing him to drop the water and yell in agony. "Ouch! Oh—help, Mom, quick! Julius is biting me."

Mom appeared on the scene and looked over the situation. "Pull him off with the other hand," she said.

As Mitch stuck his other hand into the cage, Julius released the right arm and attached himself securely to the left wrist. When Mitch tried to pull Julius from his left wrist, the bird attacked Mitch's right wrist. Mitch tried repeatedly to get the bird off, but the parrot was much too quick for him.

After a few moments, the parrot jumped to the top of his cage and walked around upside down, yelling, "Hello—hello."

Mitch jerked his arms from the cage and latched the door. "Well," Mom said, "was that enough?"

Mitch examined his red, cut-up arms. "It sure felt like enough, but I took Julius, and I'm going to make him happy. I see the water dish fell right side up, so I'm going to try to pour water into it without opening the door."

Mitch did fill the water dish. Then he shoved a saucer through the cage bars and poured birdseed into it. He had had enough of Julius for one day.

During worship that night, Mitch thanked his heavenly Father for Julius and asked Him to help him take good care of the bird. But after Mitch went to bed and turned out the lights, Julius started yelling again. "Hello, hello, hello—"

When he didn't get any answer to that,

he gave a series of loud wolf whistles, one after another. Mitch put his pillow over his head, but the whistles sounded as though the pillows weren't there.

After a while Mom came into Mitch's room. She adjusted her bathrobe belt and rubbed her eyes. "Mitch, can't you do anything about that parrot?"

Mitch shoved the pillow aside. "What am I supposed to do, Mom?" he yelled over Julius's racket. "He has food and water. I'm too afraid of him to try anything else tonight."

Mom went back to bed, and Julius changed to his *"awk-awk-awk"* mode. Either Julius didn't like his new home, or else Mitch had learned why Uncle Daryl had been happy to give him the bird.

Eventually Julius quieted down—the bedside clock said two-fifteen. Mitch fell asleep in thirty seconds.

"Mitch, wake up, quick! The parrot's loose." Mitch felt himself being shaken awake and opened one eye. He saw daylight and checked the clock. Six-thirty. Time to get up. Why did he feel so tired?

Oh, yes. Julius! His new pet. Mitch

listened. Nothing. Maybe Julius was still sleeping.

Mom shook him again, this time more violently. "Mitch, we have to find Julius. The cage door is open, and he isn't anywhere!"

Fully awake now, Mitch jumped up and checked the cage. How did the bird get out? He had double-checked the latch after Julius's vicious attack last night.

Mom and Mitch checked his bedroom carefully, then moved on to the rest of the house. As they looked in all the cracks and crevices in the living room, something different in the entryway caught Mitch's attention.

The lampshade! Where did it go?

Mitch ran to look and found the metal skeleton of the shade—and nothing more. Julius had chewed the large shade to pieces, until nothing was left except the framework and a pile of sawdust on the floor. Maybe he should call it lampshade dust.

Mitch thought it just as well if Mom didn't learn about this yet, so he moved back into the living room. Still no Julius.

Suddenly a scream shattered the silence. Mitch ran toward the sound and found Mom in the dining room. "Look at my beautiful walnut table!" she cried, pointing. "Just look at it!"

Mitch looked. The edges of the dining room table had become scalloped overnight. Chunks had actually been chewed off. And that table had been Mom's pride and joy.

Mom opened

the bedroom door

and crept in

ever so quietly.

CHAPTER

2

Julius Learns to Love

As Mom and Mitch checked the damage, they heard the whir of wings, and Julius landed on Mitch's shoulder.

Scared to death, Mitch stood perfectly still, barely daring to breathe. As Mitch looked at the bird from the corner of his eye, Julius looked huge. He stood at least sixteen inches tall but felt as light as—a feather.

Julius's bright green feathers had shown feathers of electric blue as he flew through the living room. Mitch wondered how anything could be so beautiful, yet so horrible.

Julius moved closer to Mitch's face, and Mitch leaned away from the beastly bird.

He could see Julius's bright red head and the brilliant yellow of his cheeks. No one said a word. Not even Julius.

Julius edged closer until his wing touched Mitch's cheek. Then he leaned his full weight on Mitch's face and rubbed his head on Mitch's cheek.

Mitch caught Mom's eyes. "What do I do now?" he asked silently, just moving his lips. "Tell me before he kills me."

"Move slowly into your room. He seems calm. Maybe you can put him into the cage before he knows what's happening."

Good thinking. Mitch edged slowly— very slowly—into his room and over to the parrot cage. Fearful to catch the bird in his hand, Mitch eased down to the opened door.

As he neared the door, the parrot hopped onto Mitch's forearm, then on into the cage and his perch. He looked into Mitch's eyes. "Hello, hello, hello," he yelled at full volume.

Mitch shut the door and latched it. "I'm going after a piece of wire to fasten it," he said. "I think he let himself out."

After Julius was secure, Mitch gave a

sigh of relief and hurried away to school. Although he thought about the bird all day long, he didn't tell a soul he owned a parrot.

When Mitch came home, he discovered a package had been delivered for him. Opening it, he found some dates, grapes, a banana, and a little dish with a tiny spoon. A small piece of paper dropped to the floor. Mitch picked it up and read:

Mitch,

I forgot to give you Julius's oatmeal dish and spoon. He loves oatmeal. Let him feed himself. He needs fruit too. Be sure to give him lots of attention. When he learns to love you, he'll lean against you to get his head scratched.

Take good care of him. He's special. Oh, yes, he opens his cage.

Love,

Uncle Daryl.

Mom scowled. "I wonder if Uncle Daryl

knows he eats tables. And lampshades."

"I don't know, but let's fix him some oatmeal and see what he does with that."

Mitch slid another saucer into the cage and made the mess even worse as he poured the cereal into it. Julius dropped to the bottom of the cage when Mitch shoved the little spoon through.

Mitch couldn't believe his eyes when Julius picked up the spoon with his left foot, dipped it into the warm oatmeal, and held it to his mouth. He gobbled the cereal from the spoon and dipped up more.

A big smile crept over Mitch's face. "Did you ever see anything like that?" he asked. "That ought to make up for something, don't you think?"

"It doesn't pay for the damage he did to my table," Mom said. Her lips twitched into a tiny smile. "Does it take away the pain of his bites?"

"Mom," Mitch said, "how many times does the Bible say we're supposed to forgive?"

Mom laughed out loud. "More times than we can count, but we're supposed to forgive people. Julius barely qualifies as a bird." She smiled again and poked Mitch in the ribs.

Mitch returned the smile. "Well, I think he's pretty cute, but I still have to clean his cage. How am I supposed to do that?"

Mom turned toward the door. "That's your problem," she said. "I'll be thinking about you." She closed the door quietly behind her, leaving Mitch with a filthy cage and a supermean bird.

Although the thought left him shaking, he decided to open the cage and let the parrot out while he cleaned up the mess. He'd worry about getting Julius back in later.

Julius spotted the open door in a hurry. He jumped through and took off flying. He lighted on top of the bookcase and sat quietly, watching Mitch.

Mitch edged toward the cage. Would the bird attack when Mitch messed with his cage? He watched his scary pet as he opened the door. His eyes never left the parrot as he stuck first one arm inside, then the other. But Julius ignored him. Feeling braver, he started cleaning the cage. With the spilled water, parrot seed, and oatmeal, he had quite a job. Keeping one eye on the fearsome bird at all times, he hurried and finished before the parrot moved from the bookcase.

Then he spread clean papers in the bottom of the cage, put in fresh water, and filled the feed dish. Now the hard part— how to get Julius back into the cage without harm to the bird. And without letting the bird eat him.

As he wandered around the room, trying to get brave enough to do something, he heard a whir of wings and felt the parrot land on his shoulder. Mitch stood still. He felt Julius inching over to his face—and the slight weight of the little body leaning against his cheek. Then the bright head rubbed his cheek.

It took all the courage Mitch could find to put his finger beside Julius's head. Then he gently scratched. Julius leaned on Mitch's hand, whispering, *"Kkkkk kkk,"* into Mitch's ear.

Mom opened the bedroom door and, seeing Julius on Mitch's shoulder, crept in ever so quietly.

Mitch grinned. "Well, Mom," he said,

"the Bible says humans are supposed to be master of all the animals. I'm not sure who's the boss around here, but I think Julius likes me."

A few days later, Mitch sighed as he opened Julius's cage. *I sure spend a lot of time cleaning this thing*, he thought as Julius hopped out and onto his shoulder.

The large green parrot leaned against Mitch's face, rubbing his bright-red head up and down. "*Kkkk, kkkk, kkkk,*" he whispered into Mitch's ear.

Mitch smiled and gently stroked his pet's head with his index finger. "But you're worth it, aren't you, Julius?" he said out loud. Before Mitch could get out of the way, Julius reached out and tweaked the boy's lips with his beak. Wow, whatever that was, it didn't hurt.

A recent memory verse said if you're nice to those who aren't nice to you, they'll change and be your friend. Now Mitch had proof that it worked. He had been nice to Julius when Julius had been mean to him. And now Julius had just kissed him. He and Julius were going to have lots of fun together now that they were friends.

Julius leaned forward

and yelled, "Hello! Hello!

Hello! Hello!"

CHAPTER

3

Julius Loses Feathers

Mitch finished cleaning Julius's cage. He felt so happy that he started singing. "Heavenly sunshine, heavenly sunshine! Hallelujah, Julius is mine." *Oops! That wasn't very nice*, Mitch thought. *The song says "Jesus is mine."*

Mitch knew that Jesus was his because Jesus had died on the cross for him. The Bible says if we sin we'll die, and Mitch was always doing something bad. But he didn't have to die, because Jesus had died for him. So now he could live forever with Jesus. He loved Jesus for that. He loved Jesus a lot for that.

And now Jesus had sent Julius to him.

Jesus knew Mitch didn't mean anything disrespectful when he sang about his parrot. He was just so thankful to Jesus to have his pet.

Mitch couldn't help it. "Hallelujah, Julius is mine!" he sang again while he filled the dishes with clean water and food.

The doorbell interrupted Mitch's concert, and he ran to the door, forgetting that Julius still sat on his shoulder.

"Hi, Mitch, how are—what's that thing on your shoulder?"

"Oh, no!" Mitch grabbed his cousin Cassy's hand, jerked her inside, and slammed the door.

"What was that all about?" Cassy asked, still looking at Julius. She walked over and raised her hand to touch the bird, but Mitch jumped back.

"I though he might get away," Mitch explained. "And you better not touch him," he continued, shaking his dark head. "He bit me really bad the first day I had him." He held up his healing hands and arms.

Cassy examined the still-angry-looking welts and cuts, then dropped her hand to her side. "How long have you had him?

Where did you get him?" she asked eagerly.

"I got him from my dad's brother, Uncle Daryl, and I've had him almost a week." Mitch's lips turned up in a crooked smile. "By now, Mom's almost forgiven me for bringing him home."

"I'm not afraid of him," Cassy said. Her lips pooched out as though talking to a baby. "He's too pretty to hurt anyone." Her hand slowly edged toward the parrot's red head. Julius cocked his head as the hand drew closer. Then with a small leap he was airborne, whirring his way across the room.

Mitch took off behind Julius. "He isn't allowed loose—ever," Mitch said.

"How come?"

Mitch shrugged. "Because he eats furniture, I guess. See that table?"

The linen tablecloth hung at an odd angle, wrinkled at strange places around the edge of the table. He lifted the edge of the cloth. "See? He ate the edge right off the table the first night we had him. Mom didn't like that too much."

"I see." Cassy was older than Mitch, but they were unusually close for cousins. That was because they had been together a lot since Mitch's father died four years before.

As the two young people tried to get the tablecloth back on so it covered Julius's damage, a whir announced the parrot's return. He landed on Cassy's shoulder. Cassy stiffened and stared at Mitch.

Mitch watched a moment in silence. He hadn't grabbed the parrot since Julius won the first match. He felt sure he would though, if the bird attacked Cassy. At least he hoped he would.

Julius twisted his head nearly backward as he looked Cassy over very thoroughly. Seeming satisfied with his inspection, he leaned forward and looked into her eyes. "Hello! Hello! Hello! Hello!" he yelled at super-high volume.

"Hello?" Cassy whispered shakily. Then she turned to Mitch. "How long does this record play?" she asked, her lip trembling just a little.

Mitch thought frantically. He had to get Julius off Cassy's shoulder before he broke her eardrums. Or worse. But how? Julius still had his beak four inches in front of Cassy's nose, screaming *hellos* into her face.

"I know!" Mitch yelled. "I'll get a date. He's crazy about them."

He ran to his room and returned with two of the luscious fruits. "Here, Julius," he called, extending the treat toward the shrieking bird.

Julius shut his mouth and jumped to Mitch's shoulder. As soon as the parrot settled, Mitch offered him a date. In one quick motion, Julius took the date and hopped back to Cassy's shoulder. He held the date with his left foot and soon had it torn up and eaten. The seed dropped to the carpet.

Cassy grinned. "At least he can't yell while he's eating. But I can handle the racket as long as he doesn't eat me. May I give him the other one?"

Julius finished the other date in moments and looked around the room, as though wondering what he could do next. But Mitch heard Mom coming down the stairs.

"Come on, quick! Julius can't be in the living room." Mitch took Cassy's hand, steered her into his bedroom, and closed the door. He heaved a sigh of relief.

Cassy laughed. "Aunt Fay really doesn't like Julius, does she?"

Mitch shook his head. "Lean down and see if he'll go into his cage. He's not only supposed to be in my room, he's supposed to be in the cage."

Cassy leaned toward the cage, but Julius hopped to Mitch's shoulder. He leaned against Mitch's face. "*Kkkk kkkk kkkk,*" he said ever so quietly. Then he leaned over and nibbled on Mitch's lips again.

"Oohhh, he kissed you!" Cassy exclaimed. "Isn't he precious? But he doesn't want to go into the cage."

Mitch put his index finger beside the large bird, who hopped onto it. He slipped Julius into his cage, withdrew his hand, and shut the door. "Wow!" he yelled happily as he straightened up. "That's a first for Julius and me." He couldn't restrain himself. "Heavenly sunshine, heavenly sunshine! Hallelujah, Julius is mine."

A short knock on his bedroom door was followed by Mom's happy face. "Hi, Mitch. Well, hello, Cassy. I didn't hear you come in."

"Hi, Aunt Fay. How's work?"

Mom smiled. She appreciated Cassy's interest. "Great, Cassy. Always something new." She laughed softly at her own joke. She ran the newborn nursery at General Hospital while Mitch was at school. She pointed at the huge cage that filled a quarter of Mitch's room. "What do you think of Mitch's new playmate?"

"I love him. Any time Mitch doesn't want him, I'll take him," Cassy said, only half-kidding.

Mom laughed. "If things get too bad, we'll remember that."

After school a few days later, Mitch brought Julius some oatmeal and his spoon. The bird lifted the spoon and started scooping cereal into his mouth as though he hadn't seen food for a couple of years.

As Mitch watched Julius eat, something seemed strange about the large bird. He looked his pet over carefully. He couldn't quite figure out what it was, but Julius looked different. Then his eyes fell on the bottom of the cage. Feathers! That's why Julius looked strange. A big pile of green feathers lay in the bottom of the cage. On closer inspection, he saw a couple of long blue feathers and some tiny yellow and red ones.

Terrified, Mitch went looking for Mom. He had to tell her that something horrible was happening to Julius.

Mitch opened the cage and stepped back.

Julius hopped to the open door.

CHAPTER

4

Julius Gets to Be Free

Mitch found Mom in the kitchen. "He's losing his feathers, all right," Mom said, after going to look at Julius. "Maybe birds just do that sometimes."

"No way!" Mitch insisted. "Something's wrong. Let's take Julius to the doctor and find out what it is. I couldn't handle it if something happened to my pet."

Mom rubbed Mitch's back a moment. "OK, you get the bird, and I'll get the car." She hurried away to prepare for the short trip.

Mitch turned to the large cage. Then a horrible thought struck him. How do you take a parrot to the doctor? He knew from experience what Julius would do if he tried to hold him. Could he put him into a cardboard box and shut the top? No, that wouldn't work. His pet might not be able to breathe. Or he might get away.

"Hurry, Mitch, the vet's office will be closed soon," Mom called. A moment later, she appeared in the doorway of Mitch's room, fishing in her purse for her keys.

"I can't figure out how to take him, Mom. You know what he'll do to me if I try to hold him like a kitten."

Mom thought a moment, then snapped her fingers. "I think we have a little bird cage somewhere around. Remember the canary we used to have?"

Mitch shook his head. "I don't think so, but who cares? Just tell me where it is."

A half-hour later they arrived at the animal hospital, with Julius safely inside the rusty but freshly washed cage.

"Mitch Sinclair, you may bring Julius in now," a young woman in a white coat said. "I'm Dr. Jeannie Lake. I take care of the small animals around here." She took a look at Julius in the canary cage and smiled, her gray eyes crinkling up. "Julius doesn't look very small, but I'll take care of him anyway."

When he put Julius on the examining table, cage and all, Mitch wondered what horrible news the doctor would have for him.

Dr. Lake pulled a chair close to the examining table and sat down, making no effort to touch Julius. "Hello, there, pretty boy," she crooned softly. "You look a little rough. Has someone been picking on you?"

Mitch couldn't keep still any longer. "Aren't you going to examine Julius?" he asked.

Dr. Lake chuckled, her gray eyes never leaving the large green parrot. "Are you looking for some excitement, Mitch? Do you know that parrots have a knife sharpener in their top beak? They use it to keep their lower beak razor sharp."

"No!" Mitch said. Then he remembered his arms after Julius worked on them. "Julius really bit me the first day I got him," he said, holding out his nearly healed arms for the doctor's inspection.

Dr. Lake touched Mitch's arms. "Julius only punished you a little," she said. "If he really had tried to hurt you, you would have had lots of stitches in those arms."

Mitch gulped.

Dr. Lake looked back at Julius and talked to him in a soft voice. Then she turned to Mitch. "If I needed to physically examine Julius, I'd have to sedate him, but it isn't necessary today. I already know what's wrong with him."

Mitch's back stiffened, and his mouth went dry. Mom dropped an arm around his shoulders and squeezed tight.

"Come into my office," Dr. Lake said. "Julius will be all right here." She led them into a homey room with several overstuffed chairs, and they all sat down. Mitch's mouth felt as though it were full of laundry powder. *Please, please, don't let anything happen to my pet*, he prayed silently.

"Now, I have a few questions," the young doctor said, pulling out a pad and a pencil. "Julius doesn't live in that cage, does he?" She looked from Mitch to Mom.

"No," Mom answered quietly. "His four-foot cage is too large to haul in the car."

"Good. Does he live in the large cage all the time?"

Mom nodded. "Where else would he live?"

Dr. Lake smiled. "Parrots are very intelligent and busy birds. That means they get bored easily. Julius is tearing out his feathers from sheer boredom. You must let him live in the house with you. And in warm weather he needs to be outside."

Mom opened her mouth to object, but Mitch beat her to it. "If we let him outside, he'll leave, won't he?"

Dr. Lake shook her head. "Take him out attached to you at first. After a little while, you'll be able to turn him loose in perfect safety. Oh, he may leave the yard, but he'll be back."

Mom straightened her shoulders and cleared her throat. "The only time that bird ever got loose in the house he ate the edge off my dining-room table," she said. "I can't have that, can I?"

Dr. Lake laughed. "See, Mitch? They really do have sharp beaks. Strong too. You should be thankful that Julius has a kind heart."

She turned her attention back to Mom. Her eyes softened. "I understand, Mrs.

Sinclair, but since you have Julius, I presume you're an animal lover. It's truly animal abuse to keep a parrot caged all the time, and even worse to chain him to a perch. Couldn't you cover the things he would damage?"

A little later, Mom opened the car door, and Mitch carried Julius into the house. "Are we going to let Julius loose in the house, Mom?" Mitch asked after he released Julius in his large cage.

Mom sighed loudly. "I'm not cruel, Mitch. But I'm afraid for the furniture and for myself. I'm scared to death of that beast."

"He's not mean, Mom," Mitch pleaded. "You just have to get to know him. Cassy is already his friend."

Mom thought a moment, then nodded at Mitch. "We'll try it." She chuckled. "A completely naked parrot might not be very pretty. Just let him loose when I'm not in the room, OK?"

Before Mitch could stop himself, he began to sing. "Heavenly sunshine, heavenly sunshine! Hallelujah, Julius is mine."

Mom jerked around to face Mitch; then a smile crept across her face. "I wouldn't go that far," she said as she disappeared into the kitchen.

The next afternoon Mitch hurried home from school. "Julius, do you want to play today?" he asked his pet.

"Hello, hello, hello."

Mitch opened the cage and stepped back. Julius cocked his head to one side, then the other, and hopped to the open door. Another hop landed him on Mitch's shoulder. *"Kkkk, kkkk, kkkk,"* he whispered into Mitch's ear. He tweaked Mitch's lip with his beak. Then he gave a small leap and took off though the bedroom door into the living room.

Mitch stood a moment, seeing how happy Julius was to be free. He thought about how he liked to be free too—able to come and go as he pleased, and free to say what he pleased. He silently thanked his heavenly Father that he was born in a country that gave him freedom. Mitch knew that in some countries, people can't even go to their church.

Mitch followed Julius into the living room, wondering what Julius would do in there.

Julius hopped

onto the man's head

and did a little dance.

CHAPTER

5

Julius Chases a Salesman

Mitch followed Julius, holding his breath. The parrot flew the length of the living room and dining room, then back to Mitch's shoulder. After rubbing his yellow cheek on Mitch's face, he twisted his head until he could look into Mitch's eyes. "Hello, hello, hello." Then he took another flight around the two rooms and landed on the top of the draperies.

"I don't think that's such a good place for you, Julius," Mitch said. "You could rip those drapes off the rods without even trying."

Julius sat tight and watched Mitch. He didn't say a word.

Mitch ran to get a date and held his hand high with the fruit in his palm. A quick whirr landed Julius on Mitch's wrist. He took the date and a moment later sat on the draperies again, tearing the fruit into pieces and gulping it down.

"Julius, you come down," Mitch yelled. "You're going to spill all over Mom's drapes, and you won't get to be loose anymore, and you'll pull out *all* your dumb feathers!" Julius swallowed the last bite of date, stretched his wings, and hopped into the air.

A moment later he put down his landing gear and dropped onto the front windowsill. Julius looked out the window and tried to walk through the glass. He backed up and tried again. Each time, he came to a quick stop when his head bumped the glass. Finally, shaking his bright head, he flew to Mitch's shoulder and whispered his little *kkkk* into Mitch's ear.

"Know what you remind me of, Julius?" Mitch asked. "You thought for sure you knew all about that window, didn't you? Thought you could walk right through it. Well, I guess I'm like that too. Sometimes

I get messed up because I'm so sure I know everything." Julius stood quietly on Mitch's shoulder, making no attempt to move. "Right now, you've had enough of the big cruel world." Mitch moved to Julius's cage and held his finger for the big bird. Julius hopped into his cage and onto the perch. Mitch leaned down to see Julius. "I guess we both have a lot to learn, don't we, buddy?"

Mitch let Julius roam every day for a couple of hours while Mom did something in other parts of the house. The brightly colored bird's desire to wreck things seemed to have disappeared along with his night screaming.

Mitch began to relax when Julius roamed the house. One afternoon Mitch busily worked math problems on the dining-room table. Julius exercised his mind as well as his body, inspecting every little corner of the living and dining rooms.

Suddenly he landed on Mitch's shoulder. He seemed all upset. "*Awk, awk, awk,*" he yelled into Mitch's ear.

Mitch jerked away. A guy could lose his hearing with all that racket.

The bird leaned forward, twisted his head backward, and yelled, "Hello! Hello! Hello!"

"Julius, I can't concentrate with you doing that," Mitch said, getting to his feet.

Just then the doorbell rang, and Mitch opened the door. An old man stood there, holding a tiny silver can opener in his extended hand. "Is your mother home, sonny?" he asked.

Mitch only knew she was somewhere hiding from Julius. "I don't know exactly where she is, sir," he said.

"Well, maybe you would be interested in one of these little beauties. The perfect can opener for camping." He held the tool up and gave a jerk as though opening an imaginary can.

"It looks pretty neat, but I never go camping," Mitch said, easing the door shut.

The man shoved the door wide open again. "But look how handy it would be when the electricity goes off," he said, waving the can opener in front of Mitch's eyes. "The only power it takes is—"

Julius jumped off Mitch's shoulder, snatched the can opener, and flew to the top of the drapes, yelling, "Pretty boy, pretty boy, pretty boy," at top volume. He set the can opener down and cocked his red head, eyeing the salesman carefully.

A scowl replaced the man's smile. "You get that can opener right now, young man, or you've bought it," he yelled above the parrot's racket.

Mitch stepped back, and the man followed him into the house. "Come on, Julius, bring it back," Mitch called softly.

"Hello, hello, hello."

Mitch turned to the man with a shrug. "I can't make him do anything, sir. I'll set it on the front porch when he brings it down."

The man's face turned bright red. "You can't, huh? Well, I'll get it." He grabbed a chair from the dining-room table and shoved it beside the window. Then he climbed up, putting his dirty old shoes right on the nice upholstered seat.

When he straightened himself on the chair, his eyes were almost level with Julius's. Julius did not wait to see what the man had in mind. He hopped onto the man's head and did a little dance as though scratching for food. Then he hooked his strong feet securely in the man's thick gray hair. Julius leaned over the man's face and grasped the long nose in his beak.

The man screamed, tumbled off the chair, and headed toward the door, yelling. As the man shot through the door, Julius released his nose and hair and hopped onto Mitch's shoulder. The tired parrot leaned into Mitch's face and whispered, *"Kkkk, kkkk, kkkk,"* and tweaked Mitch's lips. He gently rubbed his bright red head on Mitch's check.

"Hallelujah, Julius is mine!" Mitch sang as he closed the door and returned Julius to his cage.

A few minutes later, Mom came in.

"What was all that uproar about?" she asked. "I thought Julius was settling down."

Mitch told her about the nasty salesman. "Maybe Julius will be a good watchbird," he added.

Mom shook her head. "Mitch, you have to be careful about opening the door when I'm not right here. We live in a friendly little town, but you never know who could be at your door. You saw how easily that man got into our house, didn't you? He could have hurt you just as easily. Will you not open the door when you don't know who it is unless I'm nearby? Use the peep hole."

Mitch agreed. The man hadn't been so nice.

A couple weeks later, Mitch took Mom's hand and led her into his bedroom. "Stand right here," he instructed, opening Julius's door and holding his finger for his pet to perch on. Then Mitch took Mom's hand with his free hand.

Mom turned white. "Oh, no, you don't!" She jerked her hand back behind her.

"Mom, you're missing out on Julius," Mitch pleaded. "I want you to know how fantastic he is. I promise he won't hurt you. Please, Mom."

Reluctantly Mom let Julius hop onto her arm. He gently arranged his feet as if he understood her fear. Looking intently into her dark eyes, he lifted his wings and folded them again neatly to his sides. Then he opened his mouth. "Pretty boy, pretty boy, pretty boy!" he yelled.

Mom's eyes jerked to Mitch, then back to the large green bird. "Y-y-yes, you're a pretty boy," she stammered.

The big green parrot

nearly twisted

his red head off

trying to see everything.

CHAPTER

6

Julius Goes Outside

Mom's eyes looked wide as Julius sat on her arm, as though she were afraid Julius might hurt her. But the big bird watched her for another moment.

"Hello, hello, hello," he said, then hopped to Mitch's shoulder, touched the boy's ear gently with his strong beak, and whispered, *"Kkkk, kkkk, kkkk."*

Mom relaxed. "Oh, Mitch, he is sweet. He really loves you, doesn't he?"

Mitch smiled all over his face. "He better, Mom. He takes all my time. I'm glad school's out this week. The first thing I'm going to do after school's out is take Julius outside."

"Do you think you should?" Mom asked.

"You heard the doctor. We can't have Julius getting bored, can we? Have you noticed he doesn't pull out his feathers anymore? Well, I'm going to make him happier yet."

Mitch insisted he didn't need a baby sitter, but Grandma always came over when Mitch didn't go to school. "Just to visit," she said. "I just like to be with you sometimes."

The first week of vacation, Mitch found a piece of yarn about ten feet long and tied one end of it to Julius's foot and the other end to his own wrist. "When you learn to stay home, I'll turn you loose," he explained to Julius.

They walked outside into the shady yard, Julius perched on Mitch's shoulder. The big green parrot nearly twisted his red head off trying to see everything in the big outdoors at the same time.

"OK, Julius, you can go now," Mitch said, stopping beneath a large oak tree.

"Julius," Mitch coaxed, "the doctor said you need to be outside, so go."

Julius sat still.

Mitch waited a few moments, then gently pushed his hand under Julius and lifted him off his shoulder. He held the bright green bird high above his head a moment, then jerked his hand away.

Julius fell toward the ground like a large rock, but before he crashed, Mitch shoved his arm under the parrot, who latched on as though that had been the plan all along.

Although Mitch tried several times, Julius acted as though he'd never heard of anything called flying.

"I guess the doctor had it all wrong, Julius," Mitch said, untying the yarn from his wrist, then from the bird's foot. "You're just a little inside flower, aren't you?"

Julius leaned in front of Mitch's face, said, "Hello, hello, hello," stretched his wings, and took off flying. A moment later he landed in the lowest branch over Mitch's head. *"Awk, awk, awk,"* he said. Then he spread his wings, hopped off the branch, and flew straight to the back door. He perched on the doorknob, tipping forward, then backward.

"I'm coming, Julius," Mitch said, laugh-

53

ing. "At least I know now you won't fly away."

The next day Mitch took Julius outside again, without any yarn on Julius. Julius flew to the tree immediately this time and flitted from branch to branch.

"You look crazy, Julius," Mitch laughed. "Are you trying to be a robin, hopping all around the tree? You look more like a big green elephant to me." After a little while Julius flew to the door again, and Mitch took him in and gave him food and water.

Mitch took his pet out every day, and Julius stayed a little longer each day. One day Mitch tied the yarn to Julius's foot again. "If we're hooked together, we can go for a walk," he told the bird.

Julius refused to leave Mitch's shoulder, as he had on their first outing. Finally Mitch untied Julius, and the bird flew into the treetops, enjoying his freedom.

"Why won't Julius move when he has the yarn on his leg?" Mitch asked Grandma.

She shook her head sadly. "I think he's been chained to a perch."

"Oh, Gram, isn't that awful? When he

has the yarn on, he thinks he's a prisoner."

Grandma agreed. "People don't know it's cruel, Mitch. You wouldn't have if Dr. Lake hadn't told you." She knitted a few more stitches, then looked up with a smile. "Wouldn't it be nice if we had a piece of yarn linking us to Jesus? And if the yarn was there, we'd always go where He wanted and do only what would please Him. Wouldn't that be nice?"

"Yeah, I'd like that. But I guess that's what we do have, isn't it, Grandma? A little invisible string. But it's only there if we want it there." Mitch smiled. "Anyway, I can take Julius for walks and know he won't fly away."

Mitch took Julius for walks often. He tied a short piece of yarn loosely around Julius's foot and let it dangle. The parrot thought he was tied up tight.

One afternoon Mitch sat on the porch swing and read a book while Julius flew around the yard. The low squeal of Mom's tires turning into the driveway brought Mitch back to the real world. How did it get so late so fast? He shoved the book-mark into place, dropped the book onto the swing, and took off, looking for Julius. Come to think of it, he hadn't noticed the bird for quite a while.

"Hi, Mitch, how did things go today?" Mom asked as she opened her purse and dropped her keys inside.

"OK, except that I don't quite know where Julius is," he said, checking the treetops one by one.

"Come on in and help me make supper," Mom called over her shoulder. Grandma wouldn't take pay for staying with Mitch, so she wasn't allowed to make meals. But she got to eat them.

Mitch made a salad while Mom made the other things. "I'm worried about Julius," Mitch commented as he scraped a carrot. "He's never left the place before. Do you think he's all right?"

Mom nodded energetically. "Few people will shoot him in the city. It's against the law. I don't think he will get run over. So what could happen to him?"

Mitch thought that over. "What about dogs?"

Grandma laughed. "Dogs don't fly, Mitch."

Before Mitch could answer, he heard a scratching sound at the back door, then, "Hello, hello, hello!"

Mitch opened the door, and Julius flew straight through the house to his cage. Mitch gave him food, water, and some lettuce leaves.

"Hallelujah, Julius is mine!" Mitch sang as he finished the salad.

After that, Julius had the run of the house, except for the kitchen. And he was allowed his freedom outside any time he wished.

One day Mitch spent most of the time working outside. He didn't worry about keeping track of his pet because every little while, Julius snuggled on his shoulder for a few moments before taking off again.

Mitch mowed the lawn and weeded the flower beds. Then, not seeing Julius, he went inside to start supper for Mom and Grandma.

After they finished eating, Mitch went outside looking for Julius. "Julius! Come, Julius," he called. After walking over the entire lot, he sat on the porch swing for a while, waiting. But Julius did not come.

"Your bird either ate

or ruined every ripe berry

in the patch!"

CHAPTER

7

Julius Steals Strawberries

Mitch waited a long time, but Julius didn't come home. "Mom," he said sadly, "something's happened to Julius."

"Now don't get excited," Mom comforted. "Remember, there's very little out there to hurt him. Didn't the doctor say he might fly up to seven miles away? Don't worry. He'll be back in time for bed."

"But he's been gone for hours. Julius never does that. He checks in with me every little while. I know something's happened." Mitch and Grandma walked around the block, calling Julius's name, but no big green bird dropped from the sky onto his shoulder. Finally Mitch gave up and went home. He flopped onto the swing, feeling for all the world like crying.

Then he heard the familiar whir, and Julius snuggled close to his cheek. *"Kkkk, kkkk, kkkk,"* the big bird whispered sleepily into Mitch's ear. He tweaked Mitch's lips, oh, so softly.

Mitch bounded into the house. "He's here, Mom!" Mitch yelled. "He's just fine!"

Mom looked through the living-room doorway, wearing a big smile on her face—until she got a good look at Julius. "Mitch," she whispered, "Julius has blood all over his face and chest. Something did happen to him."

Mitch stuck his hand under Julius and lifted him out where he could see him. Oh, no! Julius's green breast feathers had turned almost maroon, and his yellow cheeks a dull, dark red. "Call Dr. Lake," Mitch yelled. "Hurry!" A large lump gathered in his throat, and he couldn't say any more.

Mom jumped into action. She ran her finger down the phone book, then started punching out the numbers.

Julius, who had moved back to Mitch's

shoulder, crowded close to Mitch's face and whispered his tiny little *"Kkkk, kkkk, kkkk."* He tweaked Mitch's lips several times.

"Oh, Julius," Mitch cried brokenly. "I should never have left you outside alone." Mitch sniffed. What was that smell? He turned his face into Julius's breast feathers and took a long, hard whiff.

"Hang up the phone, Mom," he yelled, laughing so hard he could barely speak. "I smell strawberries!"

Mom dropped the phone and ran to Mitch, "I don't understand," she said. "How could you smell strawberries?"

Still laughing, Mitch pulled Mom's head close to Julius. "He's been stealing strawberries, Mom."

Mom sniffed a couple of times before Julius lifted his wings and headed for his cage.

Mom and Mitch hugged each other and laughed a long time.

Late the next afternoon, Mom answered the door to find a round little man wearing a straw hat. "You own a parrot?" he asked.

"Just a moment," Mom said. She beckoned to Mitch, who had been reading

JULIUS

in the living room.

"The parrot's mine," Mitch answered.

"I've been looking for you all day," the man growled. He thrust a sheet of paper at Mitch. "You owe me for quite a few strawberries. Your bird either ate or ruined every ripe berry in the patch."

Mitch stood in shock, leaving the paper dangling from the man's hand. In a flash of green and blue, Julius snatched the paper from the man and carried it to his perch above the drapes.

The man's mouth dropped open; then he leaned inside, looking at the strawberry-stained bird. He pointed to Julius. "That's him! That's the one, all right. He's still stained up."

Mitch nodded. "He did it. I'm sorry. I'll pay for the strawberries. How much do you figure they were worth?"

"Ten dollars," the man said, then nodded. "Yes, sir, those berries were worth ten dollars if they were worth a dime."

Mitch swallowed loudly. He had ten dollars, but it was supposed to be the beginning of his school-clothes fund. "I'll get the ten dollars for you, sir."

Mitch returned a few minutes later, holding out a ten-dollar bill as he walked to the door. "Here it is, and I'm really sorry."

The man never got the money. Julius snatched it from Mitch's hand and flew past the man and out the door. He landed in the top of the oak tree.

Eyes wide, the man gazed at the bird, sitting up high with the green bill flapping in his beak. "Will the bird eat that money?" he asked in a hushed voice.

Mitch shook his head. "I don't know, sir. He's never had money before."

The man looked at Mitch, his eyes all soft. "Forget about paying me, son," he said. "You have more trouble up in that oak tree than any kid needs."

"Hey, thanks a lot," Mitch called as the man climbed into his shiny red pickup and drove away.

"Heavenly sunshine, heavenly sunshine. Hallelujah, Julius is mine!" The familiar song floated on the still air.

"Who's that? Who's singing my song?" Mitch asked, looking around. It had sounded exactly like his voice, but he hadn't opened his mouth. In fact, he didn't feel much like singing right now.

A green paper fluttering down from the oak tree caught Mitch's attention. Then he ran to pick up his ten-dollar bill. He shoved it into his shirt pocket and pulled his hand back just as something else dropped from the oak tree. Julius.

"Hallelujah, Julius is mine," the bird crooned into Mitch's ear, right on tune—and in Mitch's voice!

When Grandma came the next day, Mitch told her the amazing story of Julius saving his ten-dollar bill. Then with Julius on his shoulder, he started singing. "Heavenly sunshine, heavenly sunshine. Hallelujah, Julius is mine!"

Julius said nothing. Mitch did it again. And again, Julius said nothing.

"He sang it yesterday, Grandma. Honest he did. And in my voice too," Mitch insisted.

Grandma leaned close to Julius and sang the chorus. Julius sat up straight and rearranged his stained feathers. He held his berry-colored head high. "Heavenly sunshine, heavenly sunshine," he sang. "Hallelujah, Julius is mine!"

Grandma's eyes popped wide open. So

did Mitch's. Julius sang the chorus perfectly—in Grandma's voice!

Mitch sang it. Julius sang it in Mitch's voice.

Grandma sang it. Julius sang it in her voice.

Mitch sang it in a high falsetto voice. Julius sang it in exactly the same key.

"That bird can sing better than we can," Mom said later when she came home from work.

Later, after Julius had gone to bed, Mom and Mitch talked. "Wouldn't it be fantastic if Julius knew the right words?" she said. "We could take him to church and show him off."

Mitch laughed. "Sure we could. Know what Julius would say? He'd yell '*Awk, awk, awk*' at the top of his lungs until everyone went home to get away from him."

"You know what?" Mom said. "Julius is quite a bit like us. We don't try too hard to do what God wants us to sometimes. We do our own thing. I wonder if we embarrass God as much as Julius embarrasses you."

J. — 5

Mitch picked up the phone,

but before he could answer,

he heard "Hello"

in his own voice.

CHAPTER

8

Julius Becomes
a Telephone

The next afternoon Cassy visited Mitch. They sat on the porch swing playing Monopoly while Julius flew around the yard. Mitch played well and collected more money than Cassy.

A gust of wind whipped through the porch, lifting the game board, neatly dumping everything through the slats of the swing onto the floor.

Cassy laughed, then clapped a hand over her mouth. "Oh, Mitch, I didn't mean—"

A whirr of feathers interrupted her as Julius landed on Mitch's shoulder. Julius leaned his green body against Mitch's face. "Oh, Mitch, oh, Mitch, oh, Mitch," he said.

Cassy's eyes opened wide, and she pointed to Julius. "He talked in my voice." She gasped.

"Sure," Mitch replied. "Listen. Oh, Mitch, oh, Mitch, oh, Mitch," he said loudly.

"Oh, Mitch, oh, Mitch, oh, Mitch," Julius repeated in Mitch's voice. The bird looked from Cassy to Mitch, repeated his message, then flew away.

When Julius went to his cage that night, he cocked his head and looked into Mitch's eyes. "Oh, Mitch, oh, Mitch, oh, Mitch," he said, then burst into song. "Hallelujah, Julius is mine."

Mitch reached through the bars and rubbed Julius's yellow cheek, the cheek that no longer had red strawberry stains on it.

Mitch thanked his heavenly Father once more for giving him such a fantastic and interesting friend.

The next morning Mom had barely left for work when the telephone rang. Mitch picked up the receiver, but before he could answer, he heard "Hello" in his own voice. Shocked, he looked around for Julius, who sat on the back of a chair watching him.

"Hi, Mitch," Cassy's voice came over the wire. "Guess what I found in the encyclopedia last night?"

Mitch laughed. "I don't know. But did you think I said Hello?"

"You did," Cassy said, after a small silence.

"No, Julius said it before I got the phone to my mouth."

"I'm not surprised," Cassy said. "Our encyclopedia says parrots have perfect pitch. That means that a person (or bird) can always sing a certain note, like middle C, without hearing it first. All birds have perfect pitch. But perfect pitch is neater in parrots because they put it together with words."

Mitch shook his head in disbelief. "Julius just gets better all the time."

Two days later Mom picked up the phone, and Julius said Hello in her voice. Half the time after that Julius said Hello before Mom or Mitch did.

Then one day the phone rang, and Mitch picked it up. "Hello," Julius said in Mitch's voice. But Mitch heard only a dial tone. He hung it up, thinking someone had reached a wrong number.

It happened twice more that afternoon and once in the evening. Mom was puzzled. "Maybe we should call the telephone company," she said.

A repairwoman came the next afternoon but found nothing wrong.

Mitch scratched his head. "Well, thanks for coming. I hope it isn't some nut."

The young woman nodded soberly. "Yes, you never know who's out there these—"

The ringing phone interrupted her, and Mitch picked it up. "Hello," Julius yelled as Mitch brought the phone to his ear. The dial tone buzzed away. Mitch hung up the phone, looked at the repairwoman, and shrugged. "Just a dial tone," he said.

"I noticed you said Hello before you got the phone to your ear," she said. "You should listen for the dial tone before you speak. And hang up right away if you think something's wrong. Also never let a caller know if you're home alone."

"I never am home alone," Mitch explained. "And my parrot yells Hello before I get the phone to my ear."

That evening the phone rang. "Hello!" Julius yelled as Mom put the receiver to her ear.

Mom said nothing, but a moment later she smiled. "Yes, I feel cheerful tonight. Sure, I'll ask him. May I call you back? Thanks, Marie."

Mom turned laughing eyes on Mitch. "That was your primary leader. She thought my hello was extra cheerful tonight." She reached out a finger and stroked Julius's yellow cheek. "Somehow she heard about Julius and wondered if you could bring him to church and tell the kids about him."

A million strange feelings dashed around in Mitch's stomach. It would be fun to take Julius, but what would Julius do? He shook his head. "I don't know, Mom. What do you think?

"I don't know either. I'm sure it would be interesting." Mom thought a moment, then laughed. "Oh, why don't you just go ahead and do it?"

Mitch thought a moment, then smiled. "Sure, why not?"

Mom called Marie right back and told her that Mitch would bring Julius the following week. She made sure her friend understood that no one ever knew what Julius would do.

The strange phone calls continued. The phone would ring, but no one would be there. Mitch called the phone company again. As he was talking, the phone rang in his hand. He pulled it away from his ear and looked at it. The phone continued ringing, but the sound didn't come from the telephone.

Then the ringing stopped. "Hello!" Mitch's voice called from the dining-room chandelier. Mitch looked from the phone to Julius and back to the phone. "Thank you, sir," Mitch said to the man, "but I think I just solved the mystery. My parrot rings like a telephone."

Mitch stayed nearby and, sure enough, Julius imitated the ringing phone so well Mitch couldn't tell which was ringing unless he stood between the bird and the phone.

"Great!" Mom said, when Mitch told her. "Now we get to spend the rest of our lives answering the phone so Julius can yell Hello. How long do parrots live?"

"Fifty or more years," Mitch said. "He may be older than we are right now."

Two days later Mitch answered the door to find no one there. When it happened twice more, Mitch stood between the door and Julius. Now Julius was not only a telephone, but a doorbell.

On the morning he was to take Julius to church Mitch jumped out of bed early, eager to show Julius off. He had worked hard on his little speech and couldn't wait for primary.

"Let's walk to church, Mom," he said. "Julius will ride on my shoulder if I put a piece of yarn around his foot."

The sun shone brightly, and all three enjoyed the eleven-block walk. Julius clung tightly to Mitch's shoulder, his bright eyes taking in all the sights and sounds of the quiet neighborhood.

Mitch slipped into the brightly decorated primary department, but not without attracting lots of attention. Julius sat on his shoulder, saying nothing.

Finally, Mitch and Julius stood before the children. Mitch told all about Julius. "Julius is a very smart bird," he said. "He

eats with a spoon, he answers the telephone—"

"Oh, Mitch, oh, Mitch, oh, Mitch," Julius
interrupted loudly in Cassy's voice.

Mitch laughed. "I'm embarrassing him,
I guess," he said. Then he tried to continue,
but no one could hear him above Julius's
yelling.

"*Excuse me! Excuse me!*"

Julius yelled from his perch

near the church's ceiling.

The pastor stopped preaching.

CHAPTER

9

Julius Goes to Church

Mitch tried to quiet Julius, but the parrot only yelled louder. Finally giving up, Mitch went in search of Mom. He needed to tell her that he was taking Julius home. He could easily be back in time for the worship service. He tiptoed into the sanctuary with Julius perched on his shoulder. Finally spotting Mom, he eased down the aisle, passing in front of several people. "Excuse me—excuse me, please—excuse me, please—excuse me," he repeated.

Mom smiled as Mitch reached her. "How'd it go?" she whispered.

"Pretty well. I'm taking Julius home

now. I'll be back before long."

Mom smiled and nodded, turning her attention back to the speaker. Julius opened his eyes wide and looked at Mitch.

The big bird stood tall on his arm and stretched his wings. He flapped them twice. Then Mitch's heart nearly stopped as he watched his pet go up, up, up, until he fluttered in the high peak of the ceiling. Finally he settled on a light fixture twenty feet above the congregation, looking more than pleased with himself.

Mitch couldn't very well call the large green bird while someone was speaking. He knew it wouldn't do any good anyway, so he sat down to wait until after the benediction.

The sanctuary buzzed with everyone laughing, talking, and pointing at Julius, whose bright eyes didn't miss a thing.

"What do I do now?" Mitch asked Mom desperately.

Mom shook her dark curls. "Will he sit quietly through the church service?"

"Mom, no one ever knows what Julius will do."

Mom smiled. "Well, you can't get him,

so you may as well relax and hope for the best."

Mitch slumped in his seat.

Julius didn't move or make a sound during opening exercises for the church service. Mitch heaved a cautious sigh of relief. But when the first hymn ended, a new song rang through the church. "Heavenly sunshine, heavenly sunshine, Hallelujah, Julius is mine!" It sounded as though the speaker system were turned on full blast.

Pastor Arden jumped as though he had been struck by lightning. He looked frantically around, then grasped the microphone. "Excuse me," he said. "Something seems to be wrong with the sound system."

People all over the sanctuary pointed skyward. Finally, sighting the large redheaded green bird with yellow cheeks quietly swaying on the chandelier, Pastor Arden smiled widely. "Oh," he said. "I see we have a guest." He looked over the congregation. "Does anyone know our friend?"

Mitch felt his cheeks burning. He held up his hand, but only until it was barely visible above the pew.

Pastor Arden smiled. "Ah, Mitch. Tell me, will the bird stay where it is through the rest of the service?"

Mitch shrugged. "I'm sorry. I don't know."

Julius didn't move a feather until the pastor began his sermon. "Good morning," the minister said, wearing a large smile. "This morning my text is one you all know: 'Forgive and you shall be forgiven.'"

"Excuse me! Excuse me! Excuse me!" Julius yelled, putting a sudden and definite stop to the sermon.

Pastor Arden looked up at Julius. "I said," he said, completely serious, "my text is, 'Forgive and you shall be forgiven.'"

The congregation roared with laughter, and Mitch sank lower in the pew.

Julius said nothing, so the minister returned to his sermon. He had talked for less than a minute when the phone rang— loudly.

Pastor Arden jerked his head around. There was no phone in the sanctuary. The ring sounded five times, followed by "Hello!" in Mitch's voice. Silence filled the large room as everyone watched to see what the bird would do next. Mitch could tell the pastor was getting rattled.

Julius said no more. The people watched, whispered, and waited. So did Pastor Arden. Mitch drew a deep breath. Maybe, just maybe, Julius would be good now.

The minister began his sermon again. "As I was saying, we are so understanding about our own faults, but we feel quite different when others make mistakes."

"Oh, Mitch, oh, Mitch, oh, Mitch!" Julius screamed in Cassy's voice, from his perch high in the ceiling.

Once again the uproar caused Pastor Arden to stop. He pulled a white handkerchief from his jacket pocket and mopped his face. After a moment he stepped back to the microphone and shrugged. "I guess my subject is appropriate this morning," he said, with a friendly smile. "I'm sure we've already forgiven this innocent bird." He took off his glasses and held them in his right hand while he continued. "But your fellow church members may well be as innocent as that beautiful bird." He extended his arm and pointed at Julius with the glasses.

Oh, please don't hold those shiny things

81

up in the air, Mitch pleaded silently.

But Julius had already spotted the glasses. He dropped from the ceiling like a rock, snatched the glasses with his left foot, and returned to his perch before anyone quite realized what had happened.

The church remained so quiet that Mitch clearly heard Julius sawing away on the glasses. A moment later the glasses dropped onto the floor. Both pieces.

A small boy gathered up the two parts of Pastor Arden's glasses and ran to the pulpit with them.

"Thank you, my boy," the minister said solemnly. Then he turned to the congregation. "We find it easy to forgive this innocent parrot, but my friend, to God we are all as foolish as any bird. All of us. Let us forgive one another." He saluted Julius in the ceiling and sat down.

Mitch remained in his pew until everyone had gone. How would he ever get Julius down? He leaned his elbows on his knees and dropped his chin into his hands. Maybe Pastor Arden didn't judge Julius, but Mitch did. That bird was plain rotten.

Mitch's dark thoughts were interrupted

by a soft whirr of wings, and the large parrot landed on his shoulder. Julius edged over until he could rub cheeks with his best friend. *"Kkkk, kkkk, kkkk,"* he whispered into Mitch's ear. Then he tweaked Mitch's lips twice.

Back home, Julius happily rested in his cage for several hours. Mom laughed about the entire episode. "I'm sure everyone there will remember our short sermon about forgiving," she said.

On Monday, Mom assigned Mitch several jobs before leaving for work. First, he cleaned the outside of all the windows. Julius flew around the yard, returning to check on Mitch every little while.

Cassy came over in the afternoon and helped Mitch weed the garden. As soon as Julius heard Cassy's voice, he fluttered to her shoulder, leaned forward, and twisted his head around until he could look into her eyes. Then he opened his mouth. "Oh, Mitch, oh, Mitch, oh, Mitch," he yelled in her voice.

After they finished the work, Cassy suggested they walk to the corner grocery for a diet root beer.

"Sounds great, if Grandma has time to go with us," Mitch readily agreed. "Let me put Julius into his cage first."

"No! Bring him. He makes everything more fun," Cassy pleaded. "He won't be any trouble. You know he won't."

"Yeah. He's never any trouble. We know that for sure, don't we! Well, I'm putting a longer piece of yarn on him this time. If he decides to take off, he'll get a big surprise."

In a flash,

Julius landed

on one dog's neck.

CHAPTER

10

Julius Becomes a Hero

Grandma gladly agreed to go for diet sodas with Mitch and Cassy. As they strolled down the sidewalk, they met three girls. When they passed, Julius yelled, "Oh, Mitch!" in Cassy's voice.

The girls stopped and turned around. "What did you say, smart mouth?" one of them said.

"Hey, Grammaw," another yelled, "can't you make your babies behave?"

Mitch, Grandma, and Cassy ignored them and just kept on walking.

Immediately the telephone rang five times, followed by Hello! in Mitch's voice.

Cassy jammed her hand over her mouth,

but her shoulders shook anyway. Grandma chuckled aloud.

"It wasn't all that funny," Mitch muttered. "They could have beaten us up. All of us."

When they reached the store, Mitch shared his root beer with Julius. Then the three headed happily toward home with the burping bird. Julius hadn't offered to leave his shoulder perch, so Mitch relaxed and began to enjoy the walk.

About halfway home, two dogs stood on the sidewalk about forty feet ahead, growling deep in their throats.

Mitch held his arm in front of Cassy and Grandma, stopping them. "Those are pit bulls," he said. "They aren't bluffing. They can be really vicious."

"Where did they come from?" Cassy asked in a shaking voice.

"I don't know," Mitch said, "but let's back up a way, then go around the block."

They reversed direction, still facing the dogs but stepping backward. As the people moved backward, the dogs moved forward. The deep growls made goose bumps appear on Mitch's arm.

"Mitch, I'm getting nervous," Cassy said. "Should we run?"

"Never run from dogs," Grandma said. "They'll—"

"Oh, Mitch, oh, Mitch, oh, Mitch!" Julius interrupted in his loudest voice.

The dogs' ears jerked to attention, and they stopped short. Then they rushed to within twenty feet of the group and began a series of low, rough growls.

"Stand still," Mitch commanded. "Don't let them know you're scared."

Cassy stood like a statue beside Mitch. For once, even Julius kept his mouth shut.

Then the dogs eased to the side, making a large circle. Mitch, Grandma, and Cassy turned like a wheel, always facing the dogs. The dogs, still growling loudly, moved around again, coming even closer.

"They're trying to get behind us," Mitch whispered.

As the dogs circled, the people turned. Soon the dogs were less than fifteen feet away, growling loudly. Their lips rolled back to reveal long, sharp teeth.

Mitch's heart tried to come through his throat into his mouth. He swallowed several times, but the lump remained. He kept his hand on Grandma's back, turning her with him to face the ever-circling dogs. Cassy stayed right in step.

Saliva began running from the dogs' mouths, and Mitch felt too much liquid in his own. He swallowed loudly.

When the dogs were less than ten feet from the trembling people, they let out a roar, lifted their front feet from the sidewalk, and lunged.

In a flash of green and blue, Julius landed on one dog's neck. He clamped his toes tightly into the loose skin and ripped into his ear. Quick as lightning, he did the same thing to the other dog. Not being one to settle for a half-finished job, Julius attacked the first dog again, slicing the thin skin on the dog's head in several places.

He treated the dogs exactly the same until they both headed in the direction from which they had come, yelping. But Julius wasn't through yet. He rode on one animal's back down the block and around the corner, screaming, "Oh, Mitch, oh, Mitch, oh, Mitch!" all the while.

"We'd better get him!" Mitch yelled,

taking off in the direction of the uproar. The others followed a few steps behind, but soon the parrot's screams stopped, and they lost track of the fast-moving animals.

Grandma sat down on a low rock wall, puffing hard. Cassy dropped to the green grass at her feet. Mitch squatted beside Cassy, grinning as though his face would split.

"Did you ever see anything like that?" he asked. "Can you believe a parrot taking on two dogs?"

Cassy nodded, still breathless.

"What about Julius?" Grandma asked.

Mitch jumped up and held a helping hand to Grandma. "We better find him before the dogs' owner does," he said, still laughing. But Mitch stopped laughing when they couldn't find a trace of Julius or the dogs.

"I need to go home," Cassy said, mopping her forehead with her hand. "I told Mom I'd be back in a couple of hours."

"We may as well go too," Mitch said. "I'm so mixed up now, I don't even know where we last saw Julius." In spite of his worry, he couldn't stop another grin from creasing his face. "Riding rodeo!" he said, chuckling.

Three quiet people walked toward Mitch's house. Grandma helped Mitch tell Mom about Julius's bravery—and his disappearance.

"We'll take the car and search that area after supper," Mom said. "Let's eat quickly." Mom let Grandma help with supper preparations so they could go look for Julius quicker.

Mitch asked the blessing and asked for help in finding the parrot that had saved them from being severely injured.

The phone rang just as Mitch said Amen, so he ran to answer it. He put the receiver to his ear. The phone rang again just as he heard the dial tone.

Mitch dumped the phone and ran for the door. But before he got it open, he heard his voice calling "Hello" outside the door.

"Julius, come in quick," Mitch ordered, holding his arm out for the bird. When Julius had settled, Mitch took another look. What Julius had on his feathers this time was not strawberry juice! It was blood!

"Mom, come quick!" Mitch shrieked.

When Mom looked at Julius's blood-spattered feathers, she laughed. "He's all right, Mitch. It's just a little on the outside. You said he did some damage to the dogs."

Mitch carefully separated Julius's feathers, checking for injury. He didn't have a scratch! The bird tweaked Mitch's lips a few times and leaned against his face, whispering, "*Kkkk, kkkk, kkkk.*"

The tired little hero flew to his cage and went to bed. He looked at Mitch, opened his mouth, and sang, "Hallelujah, Julius is mine."

Mitch couldn't help it. "Hallelujah, Julius is mine," he sang right back to the bird.

"I never thought I'd say it," Grandma said, "but your bird really does deserve a hallelujah, or even two."

"Well, Mom, what do you think?" Mitch asked. "Have you forgiven Julius for wrecking your table?"

Mom put her arm around Mitch and pulled him close. "Mitch, your happiness is worth ten tables to me."

"Thanks, Mom," Mitch said, his eyes misty. "I love you and really appreciate the way you've put up with Julius. I know he's a real pain sometimes."

Mom ruffled Mitch's hair. "I just have one hope," she said.

"What's that, Mom?"

A smile tugged at the corner of her lips. "I just hope you still have Julius when you get a nice dining table of your own."